WHY THIS IS AN EASY READER

- This story has been carefully written to keep the young reader's interest high.

- It is told in a simple, open style, with a strong rhythm that adds enjoyment both to reading aloud and silent reading.

- There is a very high percentage of words repeated. It is this skillful repetition which helps the child to read independently. Seeing words again and again, he "practices" the vocabulary he knows, and learns with ease the words that are new.

- Only 162 different words have been used, with plurals and root words counted once.

    Nearly one-half of all the words in this story have been used at least three times.

    One-fourth of all the words in this story have been used at least six times.

    Some words have been used 11, 14 and 37 times.

ABOUT THIS STORY

- A monkey is often a youngster's favorite animal — in zoo and in story. This easy-to-read story about a monkey is therefore a special treat. It will not only delight the child who likes to read, but may also prove useful in enticing the book-shy child.

    The story lends itself happily to "guessing" the outcome, and to dramatizing additional dialogue and situations. The more bystanders — with solutions! — the merrier.

FUNNY FACE at the WINDOW

Story by SARA ASHERON
Pictures by ANTHONY TALLARICO
Editorial Consultant: LILIAN MOORE

Wonder® Books
ALLAN PUBLISHERS, INC.
Exclusive Distributors

Introduction

These books are meant to help the young reader discover what a delightful experience reading can be. The stories are such fun that they urge the child to try his new reading skills. They are so easy to read that they will encourage and strengthen him as a reader.

The adult will notice that the sentences aren't too long, the words aren't too hard, and the skillful repetition is like a helping hand. What the child will feel is: "This is a good story—and I can read it myself!"

For some children, the best way to meet these stories may be to hear them read aloud at first. Others, who are better prepared to read on their own, may need a little help in the beginning—help that is best given freely. Youngsters who have more experience in reading alone—whether in first or second or third grade—will have the immediate joy of reading "all by myself."

These books have been planned to help all young readers grow—in their pleasure in books and in their power to read them.

Lilian Moore
Specialist in Reading
Formerly of Division of Instructional Research,
New York City Board of Education

1981 PRINTING

Cover Copyright © 1981 GROSSET & DUNLAP, INC.
Story Copyright © 1970 by Sara Asheron.
Illustrations Copyright © 1970 by Grosset & Dunlap, Inc.
All rights reserved under International and Pan-American Copyright Conventions.
Published simultaneously in Canada. Printed in the United States of America.
Published by GROSSET & DUNLAP, INC.
Exclusively distributed by Allan Publishers, Inc.
Wonder® Books is a trademark of GROSSET & DUNLAP, INC.
ISBN: 0-8241-5957-8

Billy was eating his breakfast.

"Look!" he cried.

"There's a funny face

at the window!"

7

He ran to the window.

So did his mother and father.

But no one was there.

No one at all.

"Stop fooling, Billy,"

said his father.

"But I DID see it!" cried Billy.

"I did see a funny face

at the window!"

11

Susie lived across the street.

She was eating her breakfast, too.

She looked up and cried,
"Look, there's a funny face
at the window!"

She ran to the window.

So did her mother and father

and her little sister, Janey.

No one was there.

No one at all.

"Stop fooling, Susie,"

said her mother.

16

"But I am NOT fooling,"
said Susie. "I did see a funny face
at the window."

Joey lived next door to Susie.

He was the next one to see

something funny.

18

"Look!" he cried.

"There's a face at the window!"

He ran to the window.

So did his father and mother

and his brother, Mike.

They all looked.

There was no one at the window.

Then Joey cried,

"Look up there!

Up there in the tree!"

And there in the tree
outside the house,
they all saw a funny face.

"It's a little monkey!" said Mike.

"What is a monkey doing in our tree?"

"It's Bobo!" cried Joey.

"He comes from the pet store

on Market Street."

Joey waved to the little monkey
in the tree.
"Hey, Bobo!" he called.
"Hello, Bobo!"

Bobo looked down at Joey.

Then Bobo waved, too.

Joey put his hands on his head.

Bobo put his hands on his head, too.

"He seems to know you,"

said Joey's mother.

"I go to see him in the pet store,"

said Joey. "We play this game

all the time. Bobo likes it."

"Well," said Joey's father,
"we must call the pet store.
We must tell Mr. Goodman
that his runaway monkey
is here in the tree."

30

Joey's father called the pet store,

and Mr. Goodman came right away.

31

He shook his head.

"That Bobo!" he said.

"He moved so fast!

He got out of his cage.

Then someone came into the store.

SCOOT! Bobo went out the door!"

He looked up at the little monkey.

"Come down, Bobo," he called.

"Be a good monkey and come down!"

But Bobo looked very happy

up in the tree.

Soon everyone on the street

knew there was a monkey

in the tree.

Everyone came to look.

36

"See!" said Billy.

"I told you there was a funny face

at the window. It was Bobo!"

"See!" said Susie.

"There WAS a funny face at the window.

Hi, Bobo!"

Everyone called to Bobo.

"Come down!"

"Come down!"

But Bobo was having a good time
up in the tree.

"I know something Bobo likes,"

said Mr. Goodman.

He ran down the street.

Soon he came back

with a big banana.

"Look, Bobo!"

he called to the monkey.

He held up the banana.

"Here, Bobo!"

Bobo came down from the tree

a little way.

Mr. Goodman waved the banana.

Bobo came down a little way again.

Everyone stood very still.

Mr. Goodman put out his hand

to get Bobo.

Bobo put out his paws

to get the banana.

Bobo got the banana.

Mr. Goodman did NOT get Bobo.

The little monkey

was up in the tree again.

And down came the banana peel—
down on Mr. Goodman's head.

Policeman Hank came
down the street.
"I'll get him down,"
said Policeman Hank.

He began to climb the tree.

Up he went.

Up went Bobo–

to the top of the tree.

Up went Policeman Hank.

50

Soon he was right by Bobo.

He put out his hand to get him.

Everyone stood still.

Scoot!

Bobo jumped.

He jumped right out of the tree.

He jumped right on to the window

of Joey's house.

Joey ran back into his house.

He ran to the window.

"Hello, Bobo!" said Joey.

Bobo looked at Joey.

Joey put his hands on his head.

Bobo put his paws on his head.

"Oh, Bobo," said Joey,

"I am so sleepy!"

He put his head down.

Bobo put his head down

to go to sleep, too.

Then Joey picked up Bobo.

He took him down to Mr. Goodman.

"Here's Bobo," said Joey.

"Hooray for Joey!" cried Susie.

Everybody laughed.

"Thank you, Joey,"
said Mr. Goodman.
He took the little monkey.
"Come to see Bobo anytime."

"Good-by, Funny Face,"

said Joey to Bobo.

Bobo did not hear Joey.

He was fast asleep.